Based on the TV series *Rugrats*® created by Arlene Klasky, Gabor Csupo, and Paul Germain as seen on Nickelodeon®

SIMON SPOTLIGHT
An imprint of Simon & Schuster Children's Publishing Division
1230 Avenue of the Americas
New York, New York 10020

Manufactured in the United States of America
First Edition   10 9 8 7 6 5 4 3 2 1

Library of Congress Cataloging-in-Publication Data
Willson, Sarah
Up and away, Reptar! / by Sarah Willson ; illustrated by Cary Rillo. — 1st ed.
p.   cm. — (Ready-to-read)
Summary: Tommy and the other Rugrats literally get carried away by a huge
balloon when they participate in the Reptar parade.
ISBN 0-689-82631-1
[1. Babies—Fiction. 2. Parades—Fiction. 3. Balloons—Fiction.]
I. Rillo, Cary, ill. II. Title. III. Series.
PZ7.W6845Up   1999
98-54907
[Fic]—dc21
CIP   AC

Rugrats™

UP AND AWAY, REPTAR!

By Sarah Willson
Illustrated by Cary Rillo

Ready-to-Read

Simon Spotlight/Nickelodeon

It was the day of the big Reptar fair
and parade.
  Everyone was there!

"We're gonna carry the Reptar balloon, Chuckie," said Tommy.
"Are you excited?"

"Not really," said Chuckie.

"I invented this baby float,"
Stu proudly told Chas.
"See? It has a little motor. The kids sit
here—there's even a place for Dil.
Then they all can hold the balloon strings."

Stu and Chas put the babies onto the float.

"Uh, shouldn't that valve be closed?" asked Chas.

But Stu didn't hear him.

"Didi will be marching with the kids," Stu said.

"Let's go to the finish line so we can take a picture of them!"

"Stu will be marching with the kids," Didi told Betty.

"Let's go to the finish line so we can be there to cheer for them!"

The parade was about to begin.
"This is great!" yelled Tommy.
Chuckie wasn't so sure.
"Isn't there supposed to be a
growed-up marching with us?"
he asked.

Slowly the babies began to float
into the air.

"Hey!" said Phil.
"My feet aren't touching anything!"

"Don't worry," said Tommy.
"Reptar knows where we're going.
Maybe he wants to surprise us."

No one noticed the babies floating away.

"I hear a whooshing sound!" said Phil.

"It feels like we're going down," said Lil.

"I don't know about this, Tommy," Chuckie said.

"Reptar knows the way," said Tommy.

The balloon came down.
It landed on top of a big truck.
"See?" said Tommy.
"Reptar put us on this truck
to take us to the surprise."

The babies let go of
the balloon strings.
But Dil did not.

They watched Reptar carry Dil away.

"Where's Dil going?" asked Lil.

"It's Dil's naptime," said Tommy.
"Reptar knows you gotta keep moving
so Dil will fall asleep."

The truck drove to the fair.
The babies climbed down from the truck.
"I told you Reptar had a surprise for us!" cried Tommy.

"Reptar bars!" yelled the babies.
Sure enough, Reptar was giving out
candy bars.

The babies ate a lot.
Then they heard a shout.

"There they are!"
It was Stu, Didi, Betty, and Chas.
They rushed over to pick up the babies.
"But . . . WHERE IS DIL?" wailed Didi.

Meanwhile, Dil and the Reptar balloon floated gently.

Zzzzzz went the sleeping baby.

Whoosh went the leaky air valve.

The balloon landed on a train.

Kiddie Line

"THERE HE IS!" boomed Betty.
She pointed to the train ride.
The grown-ups rushed over.

"See?" said Tommy.
"Reptar just put Dil down
for his nap. He knows Dil is too little
to eat Reptar bars."

The babies stuffed their diapers
with Reptar bars.
Then they joined Dil on the train.
   "We forgot to thank Reptar," said Chucki
   "Don't worry, Chuckie," said Tommy.
                    "Reptar knows."